The Masked Cleaning Ladies Save the Day

JOHN COLDWELL

Illustrated by Joseph Sharples

•••• dingles & company

First published in the United States of America in 2008 by
dingles & company
P.O. Box 508
Sea Girt, New Jersey 08750

First Printing

Website: www.dingles.com
E-mail: info@dingles.com

Library of Congress Catalog Card Number
2007906267

ISBN
978-1-59646-868-9 (library binding)
978-1-59646-869-6 (paperback)

The Masked Cleaning Ladies Save the Day
Text © John Coldwell, 1995
This U.S. edition of *The Masked Cleaning Ladies Save the Day*,
originally published in English in 1995, is published by arrangement
with Oxford University Press.

The moral rights of the author have been asserted.
Database right Oxford University Press (maker).

Printed in China

"Let's try the song once more, your Majesty," said Billy the Butler.

"Okay," said Queen Norah. She sang,

"We're going to win the Cup. We're going to win the Cup. Ooh ah the addio, we're going to win the Cup."

"How was that?" asked the Queen.

At that moment, Captain Jones marched in. "I've just had a message from King Charles at Carrot Castle. He wants to know what color shirts our team will be wearing."

"Green, I think," said King Harry. "And his crew can play in red. Has anyone seen Princess Jane? I am going to run a training session for her after breakfast."

Captain Jones giggled.

"And what's so funny?" asked the King. "In my younger days I was known as the Wizard of the Dribble."

"That," said Queen Norah, "was because you couldn't eat ice cream without getting most of it on your shirt."

There was a crash of broken glass from the hall.

The dining room fell silent.

"What's the matter, dear?" asked King
Harry.

Princess Jane let out a great long sigh.

"Mom's right. I'm not playing very
well. I'm supposed to score goals.
At the moment, I couldn't score against
a mouse."

"On your head, Jane!" called King Harry as he threw the ball at the Princess. She jumped at the ball. The ball bounced off her shoulder into the marmalade.

"See what I mean?" she said sadly.

"Never mind," said King Harry. "By the time you've put your uniform on, Mr. Goal will be here. You'll soon be scoring dozens of goals. But now it's time for us to get to work."

King Harry, Captain Smith, and
Captain Jones loved doing housework.
Queen Norah thought that housework
was a job for cleaners, not captains
and kings. So once a week the three
men disguised themselves as the
Masked Cleaning Ladies of Om.

King Harry and his two captains
raced out of the dining room. Minutes
later, dusters in hands, and dressed as
the famous cleaning ladies, they were
at work tidying up the castle.

King Harry and Captain Jones
were polishing the cannons when
they saw a man walking toward
the castle.

"That must be Mr. Goal," said
Captain Jones.

Just as Mr. Goal reached the
drawbridge another man jumped out
of the bushes. He began talking with
Mr. Goal.

"Wait a minute," said King Harry.
"It's King Charles of Carrot Castle."

King Charles spoke to Mr. Goal
and then walked away.

"What did he want?" asked Captain
Jones.

"There's something funny going on.
We'd better keep an eye on him," said
King Harry.

King Harry and the two captains
cleaned around the castle for the rest of
the morning. But they made sure that
one of them was always watching
Princess Jane and Mr. Goal.

The three cleaners stopped for a cup of tea in the kitchen.

"Well," said King Harry. "There doesn't seem to be anything funny going on."

"I saw the Princess put the ball in the net dozens of times," said Captain Jones.

"She was heading the ball perfectly when I went by," said Captain Smith.

"There's nothing to worry about," said King Harry. "Now perhaps we can tackle the grime around the burners."

Princess Jane stuck her head around the door.

"How are things going, dear?" asked King Harry.

"Great!" said Princess Jane. "I've never played better. I've just popped in to say that we're having one last training session. We will be in the library. Mr. Goal says that he does not want anyone to come in."

She was gone in a flash.

"That sounds a little odd to me," said Captain Jones.

"Very strange," agreed Captain Smith.

"I think that it's time to polish the brass," said King Harry.

"The brass next to the library?" said Captains Smith and Jones.

"Of course," said King Harry.

"Well," whispered King Harry, "what can you see?"

Captain Jones was peering through the keyhole.

"They are sitting facing each other," he said.

"Yes. Yes," said King Harry.

"Now Mr. Goal is swinging a watch on a chain, backward and forward," said Captain Jones.

"He's telling the Princess about last-minute goals," said Captain Smith.

"No he's not," gasped Captain Jones. "He is hypnotizing Princess Jane."

"I wonder why?" said King Harry.

"To help her remember tactics," said Captain Smith.

"I still don't like it," said King Harry.

Princess Jane danced into the
kitchen.

"He's gone."

"How do you feel?" asked King Harry.

"Great!" said Princess Jane. "I feel
ready to score loads of goals."

"Wonderful!" said Captain Smith.

"I must go and work on my penalty kicks," said Princess Jane. "By the way, Captain Smith, I love your new smock."

"Thank you, Princess."

"Green really suits you," laughed the Princess as she ran off outside.

The three cleaners looked at each other.

"Green!" they said together.

"But my smock is red," said Captain Smith.

"It's that Mr. Goal," roared Captain Jones. "He's hypnotized her to think that red is green."

"Why does he want her to think that?" asked King Harry.

"Because," gasped Captain Jones, "Carrot Castle is playing in red. If the Princess thinks that red is green, she will pass to the Carrot Castle team instead of ours."

"So that's why King Charles was talking to Mr. Goal," said King Harry.

"Can't we snap her out of it?" asked Captain Smith. "Can't we throw a bucket of water over her?"

"No," said King Harry. "That could be dangerous. I have a better idea. Follow me to Carrot Castle."

The Masked Cleaning Ladies
stopped outside the kitchen of Carrot
Castle. Mrs. Jumpkins was hanging up
the Carrot Castle red football shirts to
dry. The cleaning ladies got off their
horses. They pretended to look at
the shirts.

"Oh dear," said King Harry.

"Oh dear, oh dear," added Captain
Jones and Captain Smith.

"What's the matter?" asked Mrs. Jumpkins.

"When are you going to wash these shirts?" asked Captain Smith.

"What do you mean?" snapped Mrs. Jumpkins. "I'm just putting them out to dry."

"You call this clean?" said Captain Jones.

"Yes I do," said Mrs. Jumpkins.

"It's the dungeon for you then," said King Harry.

"Dungeon?" said Mrs. Jumpkins. "What's the dungeon got to do with me?"

"That's where the last washerwoman ended up," said Captain Smith. "And she handed in shirts cleaner than this."

"Oh my," moaned Mrs. Jumpkins. "I haven't got time to do them again. The team is playing in the Cup final this afternoon."

"Leave it to us," said King Harry.
"We can wash, dry and iron these shirts
in half an hour."

Half an hour later, the King handed
a laundry bag to Mrs. Jumpkins.

"There you are. All done. Now
whatever you do, don't take the
uniforms out of the bag until the team
is ready to play. Then the shirts will
look perfect."

The two royal families took their places side by side in the royal box. Queen Norah looked amazing in her new soccer fan's outfit. She even wore a hat in the shape of a soccer field.

The crowd cheered as the two teams ran out onto the field.

Princess Jane's team was in red, and Carrot Castle was in green.

"Wait a minute," gasped King Charles. "The teams have got the wrong shirts. Carrot Castle is supposed to be in red."

"Surely," said King Harry, "it doesn't matter what colors they play in? They must be different colors, that's all."

King Charles put his head in his hands and groaned.

"Six to nothing! Six to nothing!" chanted Queen Norah. "Well done!"

"We are so proud of you, Jane," laughed King Harry. "Scoring all six goals."

"It's all thanks to Mr. Goal, my trainer," said Jane. "I must show him the Cup."

"Not today," said Queen Norah. "It is far too dirty. Nobody can see the Cup until those cleaning ladies have polished it properly."

"Yes dear," said King Harry. "I'll – I mean – they'll see to it next time they come."

About the author

I was born in 1950 and now live by the ocean. In the evening, I like to write stories and poems. I do this very quietly. Then I go downstairs and play jazz records very loudly. My family thinks that I do many weird things.  One is going up the garden every night looking for frogs, newts, and hedgehogs.